Giant
Story
A Half Picture Book

Annegert Fuchshuber

Carolrhoda Books, Inc./Minneapolis

Library of Congress Cataloging-in-Publication Data

Fuchshuber, Annegert.
    Giant story.

    Translation of: Riesen-Geschichte and Mause-Märchen.
    Two works bound together back-to-back. Title page of
2nd work has title: Mouse Tale.
    In the original German ed. Mause-Märchen appears
first.
    Summary: A lonely dormouse who cannot find a friend
and a giant who is an outcast from forest society find
solace in each other's company. Each character begins
his story from his own half of the book and they meet in
the middle.
    1. Toy and movable books—Specimens. [1. Giants—
Fiction. 2. Dormice—Fiction. 3. Friendship. 4. Toy
and movable books] I. Fuchshuber, Annegert.
Mause-Märchen. English. 1988. II. Title. III. Title:
Mouse tale.
PZ7.F94Gi   1988   [E]   87-26883
ISBN 0-87614-319-2 (lib. bdg.)

Manufactured in the United States of America

1 2 3 4 5 6 7 8 9 10 98 97 96 95 94 93 92 91 90 89 88

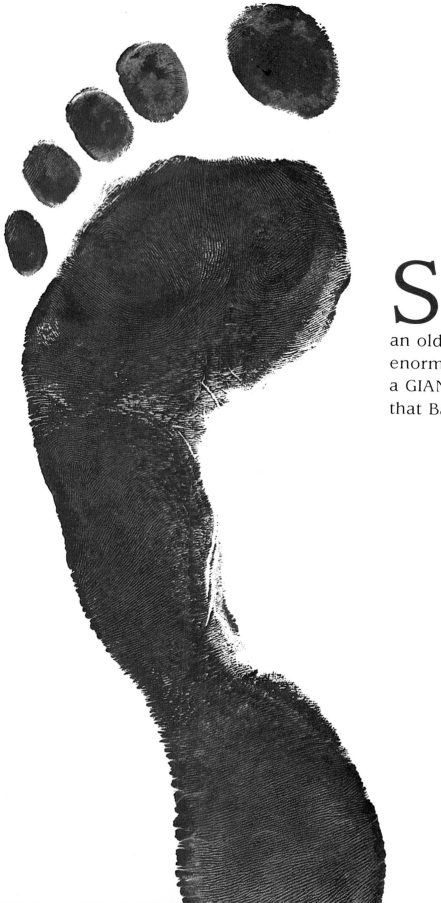

Someday, if you are walking in the right forest, you might see an old footprint. It may be the most enormous footprint you have ever seen— a GIANT footprint. Then you will know that Bartolo once walked your path.

Bartolo was a giant. He was very tall and very strong. He had giant feet and giant hands, a giant nose and giant ears. His giant mustache bristled at the end of his nose like the brush of a broom. But Bartolo's heart held no more than a drop of courage.

Bartolo was not simply afraid of spiders and wasps, like you and I are. He was also afraid of such things as dragons. Yet even the oldest forest dwellers had never seen so much as the tip of a dragon's tail in their woods.

Bartolo was afraid of everything. Night owls with their big round eyes could scare him, foxes with their pointed teeth and cats with their sharp claws frightened the giant. Once he hid all day from a gentle deer!

Another day Bartolo was scared by a raven that was following him. The giant ran away from the bird as fast as he could, finally diving into a cave to hide. But he was so big that he got stuck halfway in, leaving his bottom half out in the open.

The raven ended his flight by fluttering down to rest on Bartolo's behind. Bartolo's whole body quaked with fear, and the raven began to slip off his quivering perch. The bird quickly flew away, but it was some time before Bartolo would back out of the dark cave.

Running and hiding made Bartolo
miserable. He was always scared, and
he had no friends. More than anything,
the giant wanted a friend.

Bartolo never thought that the animals in the forest might be much more afraid of him than he was of them. But they were. All the creatures of the woods lived in fear of the giant. The ground shook under his lumbering steps, and the trees trembled when he brushed by them.

One day Bartolo gathered together all of his courage and bent to stroke a young fox. Whoosh! It disappeared into its den. Still trying to be brave, he leaned over to speak kindly to a mother blackbird sitting on her eggs. As she gazed at him with big, fear-filled eyes, Bartolo's heart began to pound. "Oh, no!" he thought. "She's going to peck my eyes out!" He covered his face with his hands and ran away.

He ran until he couldn't run anymore, and when he stopped, he found himself in a glade. Still frightened and out of breath, he lay down on the grass and cried. "If only I had a friend," he thought. "Just a small friend that I could hold in my hands."

As he closed his eyes and imagined how nice this would be, he felt something warm and soft snuggle into his outstretched hand.

What could it be?

The little mouse was tired and aching
all over when she stumbled upon a glade
that was lit by the last rays of the sun. As
she curled up into a ball, she was comforted
by the soft warmth of her resting place.
She snuggled into the warmth and thought
sleepily, "After I wake up I'll keep looking
for my friend." And as she dropped off
to sleep, it almost seemed to her as if
something were gently stroking her fur.
What could it be?

She walked and walked and saw many things as the day went on. She found mushrooms and berries, shrews and spotted woodpeckers, a big fat badger and a long black snake—but she did not find a friend. Every animal she met was polite but never very friendly. "Oh, yes," each one would say. "You're the dormouse who's so strong and brave. I've heard a lot about you." But even as they spoke, each animal was thinking, "I'd rather not have anything to do with her. Who knows . . . ?"

So one day she decided to travel farther into the woods. "I'll walk until I find a friend," she said to herself. The next morning when the other dormice went to sleep, she packed a few hazelnuts and some cranberries and left the only part of the woods she had ever known. "I'd rather have no home than have no friend," she thought as she wandered, following her nose deep into the Western Woods.

"What are you talking about?" the dormouse would ask curiously. "Oh, nothing
special," the other mice would answer.
The lonely little mouse could not under-
stand why they ignored her. She knew,
though, that none of the other dormice
would ever be her friend. And more than
anything, she wanted a friend.

The other dormice treated her with respect, for they were in awe of her courage. But not one was ever truly friendly. They often put their heads together to whisper and wonder about the mouse's courage. "She must be extraordinarily strong, or else have magical powers—otherwise she would be afraid like the rest of us." Whenever the little mouse tried to join them, they stopped talking and pretended to be busy.

She was not the strongest animal in the woods; indeed, her muscles were no bigger than threads. But she was quick, and above all she was smart. The dormouse knew exactly which enemies to hide from and which enemies to run from. She knew how to crouch, still and watchful, when the sharp-eyed owl searched for food. She knew all the dangers and all the hideouts in the forest. She had no reason to be afraid.

She was not afraid of anything. Night owls with their big round eyes couldn't scare her, foxes with their pointed teeth and cats with their sharp claws didn't frighten her. Even wild thunderstorms didn't alarm this small mouse—she actually enjoyed them.

Long ago—I do not know exactly when—a brave dormouse lived among the trees of the Western Woods.

Mouse
Tale
A Half Picture Book

Mouse
Tale
A Half Picture Book

Annegert Fuchshuber

Carolrhoda Books, Inc./Minneapolis